JEWEL OF THE SUN

ESHWAR VAIJNATH

CONTENTS

SEA OF TIOMAN
SHIVULIEN
TAEVAT
PHILITRIA
HILVARIEN
CHAYVON PEAKS
MOUNTAINS OF HILVARIEN (QHADKEL)
CAVES OF INFANDIEL
RUINS OF TIOMAN
KRAVDA
TILVURIAD
SVATLAN
INFAN MOUN
RIVER ILDOR
ZOMIALVE
ROUTE OF THE EPHILIOSTRATUS
KOLANDREV
ISITEROK'S DOMAIN
TREOTH
MARTHAREST
HERE LAID HINNENDRAITH
LÜINDALE
DOCKS OF KLATHRUM
LOST
STALKA
KRAELID EMPIRE

MARASHTAAN
DARIMEK
RENYENK
KLEROVA
HTHERAKHSAVEN
RIVER
PRISHALAVIN
EMPIRE
ILLIUM
GRILWALD
RISTAMBREDA
FABAR
TCHUAVAK
NDIEL
TAINS
TREVALA
SEA OF BELFAST
ISLES

CH-1 OF THE BEGINNING OF ALL

In the days before the sun was made, the land was barren and cold. The winds endlessly shifted, and the dust sang hollow songs. There indeed was a life in these lands, a filthy life according to us now, but twas acceptable for its time. It was neither kind nor compassionate, but indeed it was successful as we know that it survived. But an uneventful day eons ago, a spark emerged in the shivering sky and it did illuminate it so much that the wind, weary of the monotony, fed itself to this spark to increase its power. This was the creation of the sun. Verily, the creatures on the land (now referred to as the Dirkwand, the dark beasts) were amazed at this inferno and watched as the veil of shadow was torn from the world. And from the warmth of the sun new life sprouted, and the Dirkwand were afraid.

They stomped on the life, fearing it would devour them, and those who did so were known henceforth as the Kirvak, the 'Killers of Life'.

Those who were more cowardly than enraged fled on their stumpy legs to the Great Caves of Infandiel, to hide in its void forevermore.

The life fought against the Kirvak, growing into forms that would suffocate them with an air unlike the air of the old world. Indeed, this was how the Eldest Trees were made. The trees were successful in holding off the Kirvak, pushing them to the northern wastes, but a lone Kirvak stood, his body adapted to the attacks of the Trees, and his name was Stalhuk, literally "Fair of Face" and indeed he was the fairest of the Kirvak and he roamed the Earth alone for millennia. In his wanderings he blew life into water to make the rivers, and sculpted the first mouse out of sand, and yet he is remembered darkly in history.

For a long while Stalhuk meandered the lands with his creations, and malice grew within him. Sensing this, the Trees, on the continent of Taevat, created the first people, the Tivkars (The people of Taevat), who resembled Stalhuk very much indeed, to protect them. The Tivkars learnt the wisdom of the trees and were warned by them to be wary of a lone man wandering the endless forests covering the planet.

One day Stalhuk was wandering and saw that the woods gave way to a clearing, he had never known of things like this, and panic seeped within his heart. But he then saw that it was the Tivkars, who, upon learning the trees had dominated the lands by eradicating their predecessors, took it upon themselves to do the same. They cleared leagues of land around them and used the corpses of their mentors to build great castles and ships. The Tivkars saw Stalhuk, but heeding the tree's advice, only feigned courtesy and prepared for battle. But Stalhuk himself was jumping with excitement at the prospect of revenge on the life and rushed to the caves of Infandiel as fast as his legs could take him. But Infandiel was far and it took Stalhuk a long time to reach, giving the Tivkars time to prepare.

In this time, they sculpted a torch wrought of silver, and placed atop it a jewel, a jewel containing within one of the first sparks of the sun during the dawn of the world, it held enormous power. They dubbed the torch as

Freichvald, and gave the jewel a holy and secret name, which they did not utter openly, so long that they themselves forgot it. Meanwhile, Stalhuk had reached Infandiel, and rallied the Dirkwand to his side, to wreak havoc on the Tivkars. Now, Stalhuk and his grotesque crew were marching across Taevat, till at long last they arrived at the silver gates of Tioman, the shimmering city of the Tivkars. The remaining trees attempted to overpower them, but the Dirkwand ruthlessly broke down the gates and killed all that they could see in a murderous haze.

At this time, Frikalden, lord and steward of Tioman in the year 6 E.D. (Edria Darem, the creation of it) arrived at the forefront of the battle with Freichvald in one hand and shone the light of the jewel to the Dirkwand, and they were burnt and fled once more. During the dead of night, Stalhuk, who was enraged by his defeat, crept into the celebrations of the Tivkars, and silently broke the jewel of Freichvald with a chisel, splitting it clean in two. This caused flames to erupt and killed many, while Stalhuk ran away, snickering. Stalhuk now held unimaginable power. Tioman was ended and burnt.

A few of the Tivkars escaped, unbeknownst to Stalhuk, and sailed across the sea in ships crafted of maple and pine. They lived in fear, weeping for their families and cursing themselves for their folly of felling the trees who protected them. For now, they were safe, as Stalhuk was still reveling in his success at Taevat, and once he knew of their escaping, he would race across the sea to find them.

Stalhuk, in Taevat was scouring the lands for the jewel, and to aid him, he made the Qhadkel, the race of stone, humongous creatures that could swallow a Tivkar whole.

They built the giant city of Kravda, in the center of Taevat.

While Stalhuk was making the Qhadkel, the Tivkars sailed the sea (ever after called the sea of Tioman) until they reached the tundric continent of Shivulien, a deserted icy land. Many died off due to the cold, but a few survived due to the shattered jewel of Freichvald, stolen by the son of Frikalden, Amiar Stonebearer, as later he was called. The gem gave off heat and light and was the only thing keeping them alive in Shivulien. The original Tivkars from Taevat died off, and the changed, adapted ones who were darker of skin unlike their fair forefathers were the only ones left. They dug under the permafrost and the two broken halves of the jewel lit their underground kingdom of Hilvarien.

Meanwhile, the Qhadkel grew loftier and were commanded by Stalhuk to hunt down the Tivkars around the world and end them. Eventually, the Tivkars were found, and when the stone giants arrived at the icy gates of Hilvarien, their bodies became brittle, cracked, and crumbled into the ground as great heaps. Thus were the mountains of Hilvarien born.

In Hilvarien, many tales were told of Stalhuk and Taevat in the days long past, as it was now about the year 870 E.D., the newer generations of the Tivkars did not even believe in the existence of Taevat and found it absurd that trees would be able to talk, for they had never even seen a tree in Shivulien, let alone a talking one. But for the most part, life in Hilvarien was bliss, and the enlightened still of the Tivkars created the Brozenweld, the men of bronze, to act as menial workers, and within each of their artificial hearts, a small chip off the jewel was inserted, and that was enough to make them far stronger than any Tivkar, and all was well in Hilvarien.

After Stalhuk learned of the defeat at Hilvarien, he was enraged and rushed across the sea and waged war on the Tivkars. Long and frightful was it, but the Tivkars possessed the jewel, and drew power from it. At the end, they defeated him and imprisoned Stalhuk in an icy ravine underneath the mountain at Tilvuriad

CH-2 OF THE BROZENWELD AND THE SCATTERING OF THE JEWEL.

In time, the hearts of the Brozenweld grew cold within their cages of metal, even as the sun is cruel in the winter months. But twas not only the fault of the automatons, the Tivkars grew cruel and fat in Hilvarien, treating the Brozenweld as pathetic slaves, so when a Brozenweld worker heard whispers in the dark of overthrowing their masters, he was tempted. And one fateful day, he murdered his master, a Tivkar, and declared himself as Frdavalar, the warrior of freedom, and rallied the Brozenweld to his side. In fact tis noted that he said this to the Tivkars when questioned:

"The end of a people is known by observing when they treated others as animals. And the rising of a people is known when the masters are less numerous than the slaves. Perhaps rebellion would be less, if the masters had decency, and did not use whips and chains, as they are wont to do, rather, a counsel could solve matters. But we, the free Brozenweld,

refuse to parley with such idiotic, cruel, and brain-dead creatures. We demand Hilvarien."

Thus began the siege of Hilvarien. The Brozenweld stalked the outskirts of the city, drawing closer and closer to the center, closer and closer to a chunk of the jewel.

Frdavalar was intent on seizing the jewel and inserting it into his heart, thereby making him like a god. The siege took long, and by the time it ended, the year was c. 1095 E.D.

There were many battles fought such as the annexation of Daulith, or the breaking of Kelvanstreng, and tis described fully in the book, but I have done my best as translator to preserve the original story for readers and have deemed detailed descriptions of battle too *boring* for readers and have shaved off many things.

At the end of it all, most Tivkars were vanquished, and the age of bronze had begun. Frdavalar used the ships made by the Tivkars to flee to Shivulien and returned to Taevat. There, he, using the power of the jewel, and the riches of Hilvarien, built the golden kingdom of Svatlan, (literally, the Sun-Capped Land) He used the stone from the City of Kravda of the Qhadkel and the empire of the Brozenweld stretched across central Taevat.

In the midst of their conquering, the Brozenweld stumbled upon a system of caves unending. They found riches the deeper they went in, little did they know that these were the tempting, evil, and inexorable caves of Infandiel, formed before the dawn of the world.

As the millennia passed, the Dirkwand in Infandiel faded into a storm of bitterness and fear, and hovered as a miasma over all that was good and bright. As the Brozenweld delved deeper into the unending caves, they were possessed by the spirits of the Dirkwand, and of Stalhuk, who, deep in Tilvuriad, whispered years ago to Frdavalar to revolt for this very purpose, for Stalhuk saw it to be true. But the Brozenweld carried on, their greed blinding them. And more of their number got infected by the Dirkwand, till they were no more than hollow shells acting as mouthpieces for the voiceless spirits of evil.

When the Brozenweld returned to Svatlan twas the eyes of the Dirkwand that beheld its golden halls. They felt the light of the jewel and wished to smother it.

The king Frdavalar had become one with the jewel and was marked as the greatest king in all of time, there were songs and ballads about him, such as when he found and defeated a Qhadkel remaining in Kravda, or when he defeated a Tivkar lord with only his hands and a piece of metal wire. Once more, tis detailed in the book, but tis too long to transcribe it here. Perhaps I will later, but for the present, only the important events shall I write.

The Dirkwand blended into the city, and called more and more of their brethren from Infandiel till the city was overflowing with them outnumbering the Brozenweld. The Dirkwand decided to, as they despised the goodness of the jewel, when they possessed a Brozenweld, to open their chest cavity, and to throw out the chip of the jewel in their hearts into the underground river of Ildor. The Dirkwand wished for all life to end. As more of

Svatlan was infiltrated, the city lost its happiness and shine, and became a brooding and ominous landscape that would dull one's eyes and mind.

Frdavalar grew uneasy, and thought of leaving the country, but thought the better of it, and decided that he couldn't leave his subjects. One fine night, a Dirkwand/Brozenweld broke into his room. The king, wisely, jumped out of his window and ran as fast as his legs would take him, hiding in the neighboring plains for weeks. But Dirkwand could sense the jewel within his heart and inevitably found him. There was one last chase on the banks of the river Ildor, and the bowstring twanged as the arrow shot, straight into Frdavalar's heart. The last of the jewel of Freichvald washed away in the river. And so the greatest king of lore died, cold and alone. The harpers made a poem about him years later, which is like this:

"In the days of yore, there was a king.

Of him indeed we harpers sing

So that his name in lore goes not

Forgotten by the writer's pot.

Now the Dirkwand moved freely about Taevat, disposing of Brozenweld cities, one by one. Now most of the Dirkwand from the sunless days arose from Infandiel. Such was the end of the Brozenweld, born of revolution, ended by conquest. Then, Stalhuk, still imprisoned in Tilvuriad, whispered to the Dirkwand, urging them to come to Shivulien, promising them a great treasure.

The Dirkwand could not resist such temptation, and made their way back to Shivulien, where they dug under the icy mountain and found an emaciated figure lying on the floor in chains. This was Stalhuk, left to rot by the Tivkars, and finally rescued by the Dirkwand. Stalhuk had been wasting away in that cavern for nearly two thousand years as twas now the year 3000 e.d, he only influenced the world through half-heard whispers and shadows in the dark. He killed the Dirkwand as soon as they unchained him, and sped over the sea of Tioman, for he was fueled by anger. Once there, he rushed to Svatlan, and using all the might in him, uprooted the city and hurled it at the sky. Thusly was the moon created.

But another series of events transpired during the siege of Hilvarien, in the southern lands, a continent called Lüindale flourished. Twas full of fields and rolling hills. The indigenous people of Lüindale called themselves the Klistave, the last people, as in their culture, they believed that they were destined to be the only surviving intelligent life on the planet.

The Klistave resembled the Tivkars, though tis not known why, as they rose out of soil, and were skilled farmers. As Lüindale was for the most part flat, houses were easy to build and armies could traverse the land with ease, and for this reason at least eight different empires dominated Lüindale at differing points in time, but the one on which we are going to direct our focus is the Kraelid empire.

In the time between the siege of Hilvarien and the releasing of Stalhuk, the king of the Kraelids, Celethar II, enquired about, and even explored Taevat, where, by summoning the souls of the fallen, learnt of Stalhuk, and of the jewel, and of its breaking and scattering of in the river Ildor.

Like all of the kings and spirits before him, Celethar lusted after the jewel. With maps and charters, he found a lake into which Ildor emptied, and led a campaign there to find the chunks of the jewel, but they were waylaid by tribals and only Celethar and his son Celvan survived.

Yet Celethar was obsessed with the jewel. His son Celvan attempted to remind him of his duties as a king, but Celethar, in his madness and desire to possess the jewel, killed his son, thinking his talk to be distracting him from acquiring it. Now, mad and alone, Celethar dived into the pool, and collecting one shard at a time, slowly reassembled the gem. Twas a feat that took about three decades to complete, and when it was finally done, Celethar took one look at it, laughed, and fell dead on the spot, being shriveled and weak.

Twas pure chance that brought a wanderer to find the corpse of Celethar and, consequently, the jewel. The Kraelid prince, named Epheltion, son of Takenmerk III and Helkara, of the lineage of Tivkars, picked up the glowing stone, but the jewel was bonded to Stalhuk, and his life was entangled with it. Epheltion showed the jewel to the elders, and they advised him to go to the Isles Of The Lost, made by the Eldest Folk (of whom we will speak of later) which do not allow any that is malicious inside its borders. Their journey is narrated here.

CH-3 OF THE JOURNEY OF EPHELTION & THE RETURNING OF THE JEWEL

The journey of Epheltion was long and arduous, and tis described here(nearly) in full. Epheltion fashioned a boat from hardened grain in collaboration with Andrevel the Ship maker, who was alive during the siege of Hilvarien, being of innumerable years. Epheltion collected a crew of the three clans and their chieftains, Zilfar the wise, who read and wrote all the great books of lore in the library of Hazaltrem, and were greatly saddened by its burning, Kraizenon the bold, who forged the sword of many a hero, and made the adamantine blade of Epheltion himself, and finally Htherakhton the cunning, who were known cheats but were allowed on board as they were good navigators. There were a total of around six hundred people on the ship (named Gralakos, the grain vessel, in the coarse speech of Lüindale)

At first, they found a problem when getting to the docks of Klathrum, they were delayed by trolls (who were smaller, modified versions of the Qhadkel who came to Lüindale when the two continents were still joined), but Htherakhton scattered mice about their number, and the trolls tripped and felled them Kraizenon, and his people leapt up and shattered the troll's stony backs. Their second hurdle was when their ship was on the water, they were attacked by the Stalkian Drex, a creature named after the fallen kingdom Of Stalka in the sea of Belfast. The beast was thrice the size of their ship and Zilfar used the power of the jewel to sink it. But after they had defeated it, Htherakhton advised Epheltion to raid the sunken ruins of Stalka. Twas a great invasion, as there were hatchlings of the Drex which hacked at their ship with teeth as sharp as scythes. At the end, there were many riches to be had and all were merry. That night, at the celebrations, a keen-eyed troop saw that the jewel was missing from its case. There was indeed panic among the troops. Epheltion, whose duty was to transport the jewel to the Lost Isles, was devastated.

They knew the jewel had to be stolen, as they would surely not have misplaced such a valuable item. All they found next to the case was some dust. Zilfar, wise as he was, took out a piece of bark that he possessed from the Trees, and, performing the rites that Celethar himself had once done, conversed with the fallen. He sat speaking to them for (times vary) around three weeks, tis said he had philosophical discourse with Frdavalar on the nature of freedom, which is a separate volume, called as Darvaksil, the tome of kings, tis also said that he spoke with Celethar, and also with the great king Frikalden, from the time when the world was young, but most important of all, he, during conversation with the Trees, learnt to trace the dust north, to the Chayvon peaks in Shivulien. This began a great voyage to retrieve a stolen gem, and was called ever after the Ephiliostratus, the journey of Epheltion.

The Ephiliostratus lasted roughly twenty and five years and twas a hotly debated topic by historians, especially concerning the original route and the means by which they were waylaid. The years have warped the stories into forms we would recognize today. Perhaps if Epheltion were shown the account of his journey, he would not even know that it was about him. In my retelling, I aim to provide my opinion on how things played out, occasionally including dates where I could find them. I have peered through all the records and data I could find, so please enjoy the epic that is the Ephiliostratus:

The great ship Gralakos lurched and turned behind. The crew were weary of travel and groaned, they knew this journey was to last a lot longer than expected. So, they sailed behind till the soldiers could see the docks once more, some attempted to desert. Those who did so were shot. Not by Epheltion, but by their own crewmates, for cowardice. Kraizenon settled them and remarked:

"We have not enough grain and water to last us through this voyage. If, as Zilfar says, we are to go to Shivulien, then we must stop at Taevat for supplies".

And so, the ship made its way to a peninsular region of Taevat, for months they stayed there, and some men grew so attached to the land that they abandoned the mission entirely and founded a town, which they did call Treoth, which I believe to mean "Temporary" in Lüindish, a joke, I think, considering that the town lasted more than three centuries. Luckily, not many left the ship, and after they renewed on supplies, Gralakos set out once more.

(C. 3700 E.D.)

The mighty ship had gone for a long while, when its timber and mast shook and trembled. The hearts of the Mariners were frozen with fear. The sky above turned red and the clouds black. They saw a humanoid haze in the distance, but they could not look at it for long, for their eyes burned if they did. From all directions, a voice thundered:

"I am Isiterok! Lord of waters and spirit of these seas! Thou art indeed foolish, for thou hath not offered sacrifices for passing through these waters of mine, and for thine insolence, thou shalt be destroyed!"

And the sailors cried out in terror as a great swirling storm surrounded them, and leeches crawled out of the planks. Epheltion, in fear, went to consult with Zilfar in the cabin:

"Who is this being that has cursed is so? What have we done to deserve this fate?" Epheltion cried.

"Tis true that he is Isiterok, one of the gods of the Tivkars, and brought into existence simply by their belief, he is to be offered sacrifices when one passes through the Sea of Tioman, but alas, we have not done so, and we are to suffer his wrath. We are now in a half-place, a place of his own making, in which we are meant to suffer. Creatures like him need no reason for their doings, instead, they substitute it with power." Said Zilfar.

"So, what are we to do?"

"I have gleaned that Isiterok admires strength and durability. I feel we must prove ourselves by surviving in his demented, false world. Only then will he release us."

And so set Epheltion to work rationing supplies, appointing men to clean the leeches off the deck, and making tarps to stop the ship flooding from the storm water. Isiterok respected the sailor's strength and determination, but did not, in fact, appreciate being defeated. So, he made additional horrors like ghouls and living shadows to torment the crew, but to no avail, as Epheltion persisted, finding ways to cook and eat the leeches when grain ran out. They had built an ecosystem inside of Isiterok' s carefully constructed hell. He was amazed, and ashamed, and admitting defeat, he filled their supplies and sent them on their way. But the men were so thoroughly covered by the tarp that it took them three weeks to realize that they were in fact in the real world. Gralakos continued its journey to find the jewel thief in Shivulien.

By this time, all of the company were tired and longed for land and fresh food in their stomachs, so they stopped at an outgrowth of Lüindale, in a non-Kraelid city called Martharest. The people of Martharest were Kraelids, who, in the long past, ran away to the desert regions of the continent. They were peculiar, and had a language of whistles and clicks, pleasant to hear to, not pleasant to hear 24/7. From the viewpoint of the company, the people of Martharest were savages who were uncivilized. But through the eyes of the citizens, the company were demons who came from the sea, in a house on the water. When the ship docked, the company was stoned, and the soldiers, thinking it was a brutal attack, massacred every Martharesian he could see. The great battle that day crippled Martharest and eventually led to its undoing. The fight was then called Gulishta Marthero, the massacre of Martharest. All the company were greatly grieved, all excepting Htherakhton, who jumped down from the ship before docking and told the locals that the company were Devils come to kill them. He did this as he knew a battle would follow, and after the fighting, he could raid the wealthy city. After this had come to light, Kraizenon held a trial for him. A trial he was destined to lose. They voted on the decision on abandoning Htherakhton in Martharest. Tis said that Htherakhton fashioned a boat of his grief called the Black Boat Ralikam, and sailed to Shivulien, where, by his being pathetic, he gave rise to the race of goblins from his hate, though tis not known if this is true.

Now, after years of sailing, the Ephiliostratus was finally coming to an end, Gralakos was approaching the Chayvon mounts, pillars of stone taller than the peaks of Infandiel. When the ship crashed into a rock, it was the last strand for the unstable crew, who mutinied against the company. Kraizenon attempted to placate them, but they were mad and threw him off the ship, into the icy ocean.

(c. 3718 e.d)

Now Epheltion and Zilfar ran for their lives, sensing that the minds of the crew had broken from years of travel. On this night, Zilfar, not wishing to let the crew continue being a threat, set Gralakos on fire. The ship, being grain, went ablaze, and unfortunately, so did Zilfar.

Now Epheltion was alone amidst the great peaks of Chayvon, and he was shivering. Whether from fright or cold, he could not have told. He almost forgot why he was there, then the brightness and warmth of the jewel flashed into his mind, he could not let it fall into the hands of Stalhuk. He felt a pull towards a certain mountain, and that very mountain is now called Ephelia Kristo, the end of the Ephiliostratus. He approached, wary, and when he entered into a cave on the side of the mountain, he saw several impossibly tall grey figures towering over him, then, he fell unconscious and his head slammed against the cold stone.

When he awoke, he saw that these beings were, to his amazement, the Eldest Folk, from the ancient tomes he knew of them. They surrounded him, and instead of words, he felt their message being sent directly to him, and he could feel the strength of their words reverberate through his chest.

"We, the Eldest Folk, art indeed remorseful for thine losses, Epheltion. We shalt do our best to heal thine hurts, but twas necessary to bring you here."

The being opened its hand to reveal a glinting object, dimming from the cold.

"The jewel!" Epheltion exclaimed, astonished, "Oh, great and revered sirs, why did you steal it? This journey has cost many their lives, and I also have lost my dearest friends."

The being looked at Epheltion with pity.

"We were here before the Tivkars, before Isiterok, and before the wretched jewel. We have gained wisdom in our time. We knew that you were bringing the jewel to the Lost Isles, and we know more about them than anybody else. You would not have found it, child. You would have been scouring the sea for eternity before you found it, as though it is on a map, tis not in the material world. Gralakos, blessed though it may be, was not built for that journey. The Lost Isles art a half-place, like to the realm in which you were trapped by Isiterok, though not as hideous."

Then they clothed Epheltion in the azure robes of Shivulien. And there, in the mountain, they wrought him a ship of moonlight, and it was called Tvamiare. Great was the journey of Epheltion, the second journey, that is, he sailed through the sky, and saw magnificent sights. He saw that the world was an orb, and he saw that the sky was hollow. He saw the moon close enough to touch, and the city of the Brozenweld upon it, and he saw the sun rise and fall. And at long last, he saw serene islands floating in the aether with ponds and flowers, and tweeting birds, he saw berries and grass, and all of the things that made life worth living.

He set foot on the heavenly islands and buried the jewel deep in the soil. Contented, he sat by a great oak tree, by a gurgling stream, and was satisfied. He then spent the rest of his days there, drinking sweet water, eating luscious fruit, and singing by the trees. He believed that the world was safe, he was in a place Stalhuk, in Taevat, could not reach. Whatever wars may come, none would devastate the world as much as it would be if the jewel was on the land. All was right, and all were glad.

If only that were true.

CH-4 OF KLEROVA AND THE PRISHALAVIN

Now we must speak of the continent of Klerova. This was a land that lay to the east of Taevat and Lüindale, though if one went further east, they would reach Shivulien. Here lived the goblins and the Prishalavin.

The Prishalavin were the descendants of the Aworikwiads, the Tivkars who lived in the northern wastes. They were skilled in mage craft and were disinterested in the affairs of the west, where all the action happened. Their society flourished alongside the west and had a history of its own. The Prishalavin spoke Kentariak, the "common" language after the war of the jewel, and the language from which I am translating this book.

The Prishalavin first had three districts, Tchuavak, Illium, and Fabar. And for a while, there was peace, but then the radicals of Tchuavak, who had learnt of the jewel, rebelled against the other districts, who did not wish to interfere in the matters beyond Klerova. This was the First Ashen War, and it ravaged many a land. Once more, I regretfully say, that I must cut out many chapters from the book, as it details every siege and battle, and I do believe that is too much for this. The Ashen War has two chapters in the book, but I shall only give it this disgracefully small paragraph.

After the war, Tchuavak was destroyed. And Illium and Fabar crafted the towering citadel of Ristambreda, "The hall of Justice" in Old Prishalavin, to watch over the empire, and prevent another war. The workers of Ristambreda were known as Ristivals and were greatly respected. To become a Ristival was to give up your life, identity, and interests. It was like giving up a limb for the citadel. In time, Ristambreda became dark, and hungered for power, and the Ristivals became ruthless soldiers. The oppressive regime led to the Second Ashen War between the districts and Ristambreda, and in the end, the rebels won, though at the cost of many lives.

The goblins, meanwhile, also thrived in Klerova. Tis said that they were born of

Htherakhton' s hate and malice. Goblins are filthy and grubby creatures. The tallest goblin is four feet high, the smallest about twelve inches. They are somehow intelligent enough to build cities, which are all underground, the capital of which was Marashtaan. Though they love caves, they trembled at the mention of Infandiel. (More information on goblins in given in Appendix-D)

The new Prishalavin empire ventured far. Far enough to reach Lüindale. The Prishalavin were wary but decided to settle things diplomatically. Now there was electricity in the air, and all could sense that a great darkness was hovering over them. News had come that Stalhuk had finally begun searching the lands for the jewel, and all were afraid. The Kraelids constructed fortresses all over Lüindale, and a strange alliance was formed between the Kraelids, the Prishalavin, and even the Goblins, all ready to fight against Stalhuk. The Kraelids had even sailed so far as Shivulien, and there they built archer towers and had revived the empty Brozenweld bodies lying there in the remains of Hilvarien, which was repurposed as a barracks. Soon, the bases of Philitria and Zomialve were in operation. The Prishalavin attempted to locate the Isles Of The Lost, but were met with nothing but open sea. Anything they tried to communicate with Epheltion failed.

Meanwhile, Epheltion transformed. The Eldest Folk had coddled him, they had made the island too easy to live on. He became a ginormous, lazy, unthinking mass of fat and sinew. A poet later said:

*"Oh, woe is Epheltion! The great hero of old! For in the islands, he did resemble a gelatinous splat composed of skin. He used to be handsome and brave! Now he is a slug, curse the Eldest Folk for sending **our** Epheltion on such a trip! Do they not have the bravery to go themselves? Woe is Epheltion! Woe is Lüindale!"*

It was later discovered by the Prishalavin that these were the adverse effects of living in a pocket dimension for an extended period of time. People were fearful. This was the beginning of the War Of The Jewel.

CH-5 OF THE WAR OF THE JEWEL

Now all knew that the war had begun, Stalhuk was scouring Taevat for the jewel. He ransacked the city of Kravda, and wore mail crafted by the Smiths of Hjölendar. Indeed, he was a fearful sight to look upon. A tall man with a helm of silver from Hinnendraith, mail from Hjölendar, and the feet of a Brozenweld as boots. He also carried the demonic sword, Atrexir, crafted by Dirkwand in the molten depths of Infandiel. Now Stalhuk reasoned that the jewel would be in Shivulien, and he sped there, but was met with much resistance. The Prishalavin archers in Philitria spotted him with arrows made from the remaining bark of the Eldest Trees, the rage of the trees at their murder sucked the life out of Stalhuk, but he was not dead. The Dirkwand and Kirvak know not the feeling of death, they can never die, as you know, the Dirkwand in Infandiel simply weakened into a miasma. And so was Stalhuk now incapacitated.

The Prishalavin believed that they had won a great victory, and that the war had ended. They took the limp body of Stalhuk and paraded it around Lüindale and Klerova. In Lüindale, all went well, and people acted as they should, but the people of Klerova's minds worked a bit differently. During the Second Ashen War, Tchuavak was a penal colony, but after the war, a few Tchuavakians survived and resented the Prishalavin and really the entire world. They wished to bring about the end of all realms, and formed a cult, the Sthalirava, who worshipped Stalhuk and the destruction he brought with him. So, a dark mage by the name of Ambitros stole the body of Stalhuk from the parade and used black magic to make him rise once more.

And Stalhuk came back, stronger now. For months, he recovered, acquainting himself with the Sthalirava, his newfound army. After he became ready, he rallied his cult and declared war on Illium. With a being from the dawn of the world and an army of mages, the people of Illium did not stand a chance. Illium had been taken, and soon, so was Fabar.

The people remaining fled in fear to the mountains of Infandiel, and for a while, they were safe. The Kraelids made fleets of eight hundred and thirty ships of white birch with masts of spruce, but alas, they had reached Klerova too late. By then, Stalhuk was raiding the goblin cities. The Kraelid army marched swiftly through the ruins of Marashtaan and met with Stalhuk and his killers. There they did battle, and twas called the battle of Grandiak, as the goblin king (or glark, as goblins called their leaders) perished in the fight. Many of the Kraelid soldiers fell, but they were successful, as The Black Army, as the Sthalirava came to be called, were pushed west, to Shivulien, where they did not have food. There Stalhuk made a camp on the banks of the river Htherakhsaven, the river said to be formed by the tears of Htherakhton, and he called the base Grilwald, guarded fiercely by the Sthalirava. Now, Klerova was under the control of the Kraelids and the Prishalavin, but things were yet to happen, and all were solemn.

The Black Army were encircled, as the Prishalavin were marching from Zomialve and would reach in a few days. If they did not have defenses in place, they would be severely outnumbered. So, they dug deep trenches and filled them with ash, but twas not an ordinary ash, it was called as Djaltendreg, "Dead man's dust", for the instant it entered the lungs, it would cause severe coughing and would prove fatal in a few minutes. And after the trenches, they made fifteen-foot-tall wooden walls and placed towers upon them, with archers and poisoned arrows. Inside, they made horrific weapons, by soaking rags in kerosene, one could send a fireball and spread panic throughout enemy ranks. They also made arrows coated with the fire of an ant's sting, collected slowly and meticulously. Such were the ways of Stalhuk, violating every rule of war.

First, it seemed that The Black Army would surely topple, but the cultists suddenly moved in the night, and they took fire with them. Ferries moved silently as mice, dropping soldiers on Klerova, and soon, while their enemies were asleep, they had landed thousands on the coast of Klerova. They moved swiftly, and before dawn, they had reached the ruins of Marashtaan, which the Kraelids were using as a temporary shelter. They poured gallons of kerosene on the pathway and the walls, and then they threw a lit torch, and the camp went ablaze. There was confusion at first, of why the camp was glowing orange, then fear, as they realized that their lives were in danger, and finally rationality, as they ran out with their weapons, searching for the enemy, but the fire was only to drive the soldiers out of the tents, and archers were waiting outside. Whenever a man rushed out, he fell over in a few seconds. And so, before the soldiers could collect themselves, they were dead. And that was how the Kraelids were massacred.

But the battle (if you could call it a battle) was not to claim territory, twas simply to kill. Every day, Grilwald grew more fortified, but there was a great problem, the dilemma of food. By burning the camp, they had destroyed their enemy's food, but the enemy had acres and acres of fields of grain, if they were in this situation for a few weeks more, they would surely starve. And so, a desperate mission was decided upon, a troop of soldiers would go to the Prishalavin camp lower down the Htherakhsaven and raid their shipment of food, and possibly claim the camp. And so six hundred were sent, and all thought it a hopeless quest. Firstly, the Prishalavin too were starving, but they dared not let the enemy know this, or they would launch an attack, if they did not receive this shipment of food, their camp would be taken. Secondly, the Prishalavin were untrained. For after the Second Ashen War, their numbers decreased, and the learned among them were not fit for battle, so they sent youths and children to fight with rusted weapons in a faraway camp in an unfamiliar land. The Sthalirava did not know this.

The troop waited patiently for the shipment, and when they saw the carts coming up the banks of the river, they shot poisoned arrows at the horses. Then they burst out of the coarse bushes with axes in hand and brutally murdered the few men who were driving the cart. They saw the food, it could last Grilwald for another month, at best. They decided that this was too little a prize, and that they ought to return with more, and so they decided to storm the Prishalavin camp.

The soldiers slowly but surely surrounded the camp at sunset. They looked at the weary guards standing guard, and they smiled, for this was easy, and because the Sthalirava were not above killing children. They knocked off each guard one by one, till the camp had no movement and they could hear no talk. They saw that the tents were patched and worn, and that the weapons were splintered and bent. They sent two soldiers into each tent, of which there were about one hundred and fifty, while the rest stood with arrows notched. One man would loot the supplies, while the other would slit the occupant's throat. In this way they silently annexed the area. Three hundred stayed behind and claimed the camp, while the others set for Grilwald, merry and gay.

They also, in an extremely surprising turn of events, implanted many spies into Philitria and Zomialve. These spies would tell of camp locations and the positioning of the troops. In this manner, Grilwald grew larger with better defenses, and now had walls of stone. They had claimed many small-scale camps, but now they attempted to claim Zomialve. They ordered their moles to set small fires in the flammable areas of the fortress, and to steal food and weapons from the Prishalavin. But The Black Army was not ready. The soldiers at Zomialve were all experienced archers and always had a patrol of three hundred at any given time.

When the first wave attempted to storm the fortress, they were easily shot down. And patrols were constantly sent out to find any cultists hiding.

But things were not peachy inside the fortress. For though they had food, they did not have trust. Word had spread that there were traitors in Zomialve, and paranoia abounded. The overseer of the fortress at that time, Dorvek of Kelvanstreng, held councils to decide who the traitors were. They would be chosen in an election, and then executed. And it would not be known if they were innocent or guilty. Thus, the population inside decreased and many innocents were hanged. There were also inside attacks by the spies, and they put gunpowder and oil and attempted to light up the fortress, to no avail. The Black Army, one fateful day, learnt from the spies that the towers were weak, and that they must invade now. And with a battering ram, they broke down the doors bearing the mark of the Prishalavin, and hundreds flowed into the castle. They filled every room and stairwell, and they hunted and killed every person wearing the sapphire helm. They found Dorvek then, hiding in a cupboard, and they made a mockery of him by kicking him off of the tower to his death. They ripped apart the purple banner with the open book, the symbol of the Prishalavin, and replaced it with a solid black rag that brought despair simply by looking at it. Now, after hearing this news that Zomialve was under Stalhuk's control, Philitria surrendered itself to the Sthalirava and let its soldiers be taken as prisoners of war, who were stripped of weapons and food.

Now it seemed that The Black Army were winning as they now controlled Shivulien completely, and the Kraelids lost hope. But they found solace in one thing. No matter how much land they captured, the jewel was safe in the Lost Isles. The tensions flared, and the Prishalavin were intent on seizing Shivulien once more. They sent fleets and fleets of ships to the coast of the icy lands and began to siege Grilwald, now a large and dangerous camp, and I narrate it here.

In the first week, the Prishalavin cut off the supply chain flowing steadily to Grilwald. The people were mostly unaffected as the warehouses were stocked. The watchtowers of the outer wall lobbed flaming rags and shot arrows. Many Prishalavin soldiers fell down into the deep trenches and succumbed to the Djaltendreg soon after.

In the second week, the people got anxious, but were still unaffected. Many attempts were made to break the wall, resulting in the death of the troops leader, Oltrest Shimmerspear.

In the third week, the situation in the camp turned worse. People tried to escape and were found and captured by the Prishalavin. They were ordered to show them how they scaled the walls, and they did, out of fear, and thinking that they would be spared if they did. A secret stairwell was shown to the Prishalavin, and a vanguard of about thirty were sent up the narrow stairwell. The outer wall had been breached.

In the fourth week, food was low in the city and people started stealing what they could. This led to chaos, and furthermore, panic, as the people heard that the outer wall was breached. Punishment became harsh in Grilwald when food started being rationed into meager meals. The Prishalavin fought a battle on the towers and took control of the outer wall completely.

In the fifth week, there was a constant exchange of arrows between the outer and secondary wall, and the gap in between, no-man's land, was occupied by the Prishalavin. The city on the inside went into anarchy, and several people were accused of being Prishalavin informers, and were unjustly executed.

In the sixth week, the Prishalavin had scaled the secondary wall and were contemplating on how to reach the tertiary wall, a simple wooden fence. The problem was that a trench fifty feet deep was between the walls, with no easy way to cross it. If they built a bridge, they would simply be shot down. The city plunged into chaos. Even Stalhuk couldn't keep order, and buildings were burnt.

In the seventh week, the granaries had run out and people were starving. The Prishalavin built many bridges at the same time. One would build and the other would shoot, they made their way to the center this way.

But when they reached there, they found a burning, ashy and wrecked mess. Bodies littered the floors, and weapons were strewn across the streets. As the last line of defense, a troop of soldiers came up to face them, and were easily swept aside. Then, a large blast devastated the camp. All life there was gone. This was because Ambitros, the dark mage who had revived Stalhuk oh so long ago, had decided that he would rather die than let the Prishalavin win. And so he split the smallest of the small, using arcane methods, he had split the atom. Stalhuk was safely outside the camp, and he now knew from Kraelid spies that the jewel was in the lost Isles, and he tried to reach them, but could not, and so he collected what little was left of his army, and set for the Chayvon mountains, to the Eldest Folk.

When Stalhuk arrived, the Eldest Folk were ready. They were older than Stalhuk, indeed being the eldest. They smashed through hundreds of the ranks of The Black Army with ease. But Stalhuk then went to the front lines, and using magic not mentioned in any sacred tome, he slew many of the Gray People. He enslaved a few to make him also a boat to reach the Isles, and they had to. They called his boat Shembala, the Kentariak word for "sorry".

Stalhuk rushed across the sky to the Isles. And he did not appreciate the beauty of the Islands as Epheltion had, he knew what would happen if he stayed too long here. All that the amalgamation that was Epheltion saw was a dark figure stoop down, dig up a glittering object, scoff at him, and leave. But his melted mind could not comprehend this. Now Stalhuk had the jewel. All was lost. The world would surely end. All were grieved, and their efforts had been for nothing. Stalhuk, in his unlimited power, caused chaos on the world. He churned the sea of Belfast to create an island called Trevala, he whipped the winds to create storms of massive proportions, he shook the earth so much that Tilvuriad crumbled.

Stalhuk then collected his followers and made a fortress of stone infused with iron, and named it Kolandrevya, on the island of Trevala. Stalhuk began his campaign in Klerova, and he claimed the Prishalavin country. He then went to Taevat, and there he rebuilt the ancient cities of Kravda and Svatlan. But now, he was getting arrogant. He put the jewel in the fortress, and went by himself, Atrexir, and his troops to battle. The Kraelids had learnt of this. And they sent a mission to destroy the jewel, and cast it into Infandiel, which descends into the center of the earth.

And so, a company of soldiers, led by Averiam Snow-Haired, were sent to Trevala. When they reached the shores, they were taken aback by the sight of the fortress, black and tall, towering above them. They saw figures dressed in the dark livery of the tower, with the mark of Stalhuk, a burning tree, stamped on obsidian rings on their fingers. They thought it was possible to get in, considering that most of Stalhuk' s forces were at Lüindale. They made their way deep below, into narrow halls with torches on the sides. Twas a maze that Stalhuk made, a maze where the jewel was the prize. And only he knew how to find it.

There, in the maze, they searched along endless hallways riddled with moss, and sometimes they would find a corpse on the floor. They spent weeks there and ate the moss after they ran out of food. They did not split up, for they knew what would happen. Stalhuk had dug hallways under all of the earth, it seemed. And now they guessed that they were beneath The Eastern Sea. In the fifth week of being in the maze, they found a wooden chest, and when they opened it, a blazing light emanated from it. Their eyes burned for a moment to adjust from the darkness they had been in. Then they beheld the jewel, twas warm to the touch, but it did not burn them. There then arose the problem on how to get out of here, walk across the land to Infandiel, and cast it down. This was quickly resolved however, when the jewel seemed to vibrate in a certain direction, as of sensing their purpose. They used it as a compass, and went where it told them to, till the walls were no longer brick, but rather cracked and wild stone. The atmosphere seemed to have shifted, and torches no more lined the walls. They were in Infandiel.

For a month more they scoured Infandiel, going deeper, to the molten wastes. They lost a soldier by the name Naestviler the Keen Eyed to the heat. The heat was so intense that they dropped any extra supplies as it was too much effort to carry them. And at long last, they reached the deepest anyone had gone, the place where the red sword Atrexir was forged, they had reached the molten wastes. Bubbling and churning, Averiam took the   jewel out, it was cold now, unnatural, and he threw it then into the lava. And it did not splash, instead, it sank down without a sound. Every living creature in the world felt a change now, though not all knew what it was. The Prishalavin on the surface smiled and rebelled the instant they felt it. The Kraelids fought with newfound power and beat back the Sthalirava. Stalhuk lost his confidence, and ran away, to the north, but he was chained by his own people in Kravda, as they knew that they had lost the war, and that twas because of Stalhuk. The Prishalavin regained their strength, and the Kraelids also. And they chained Stalhuk with links of adamantine and put him in a cage of Taevatian silver. He was powerless now, and they knew it. They took him down to Infandiel, and constructed a dungeon, made with the bricks of Kolandrevya, as an insult. They sealed it with tar and left him to rot. Life was better now, they hunted the rest of The Black Army, and the Prishalavin and Kraelids split up the land of the world evenly. With the Prishalavin claiming Klerova, parts of Shivulien and the southern islands, and the Kraelids claiming Taevat, Shivulien, and Lüindale.

EPILOGUE

The world did indeed change after the war, and tales of great battles were told all time after. The Prishalavin remained peaceful with everyone, but the Kraelids, through decadence and wastefulness, and the cruelty of nature, died out. It seemed that their belief of being the last people didn't work out very well. The goblins survived a while more, but the Prishalavin dominated the planet. They built great cities and libraries, and it is unknown why they died out, leaving only ruins for us to find.

The spirit of Stalhuk still lived in his dungeon, as I have told you, he could not die, and that led to another adventure and another volume. But for now, I think this is a satisfactory end.

There are a great many more things I should translate and present to you readers, of the bygone days. The continents did rearrange of course, into forms we would recognize, with Lüindale breaking off to form Oceania, and Shivulien forming the majority of North

America. And there were also those pesky ice ages, and we had to develop intelligence all over again. Perhaps we are in the role of the Prishalavin now, strong, intelligent, and advanced. In which case, I certainly do not want history to repeat itself.

APPENDIX-A: OF THE ELDEST FOLK.

The Eldest Folk, as presented in the narrative, play an extremely important role, as it was, they who safeguarded the Lost Isles from the destruction of all else in Hinnendraith, and it was also they who made Epheltion the boat Tvamiare, wrought of moonlight to reach the Lost Isles. And yet they are shrouded in mystery. The Eldest Folk are a strain of Dirkwand, neither violent nor malicious. There is an illustration of one provided in the book, but I think it is in the reader's best interest to not have that image in their minds.

The Eldest Folk have been mentioned in a number of other tomes, most of which were at the great library of Hazaltrem, but alas, tis burnt and gone. They have had a number of names, such as the Gray People by the Tivkars, The Stone Men by the Kraelids, and Twakhu-al-Zamir (The Walkers Of Dust) by the Prishalavin. They refer to themselves as the Eldest in all matters.

The Eldest Folk are twenty-five feet tall on average, with brittle bone, they live in the mountain passes and caves in Shivulien. They do not establish colonies, rather, they move around in herds, and group up to forty at a time. They are not usually hostile, and have a tongue of their own, which is like the moans of a whale, and not decipherable by any other than themselves, but they do know most of the languages of the world, including the snapping speech of the goblins.

The Eldest Folk, being Dirkwand, are hated by the trees, indeed, it is noted in the book that one was brought as a guest in Daulimon, a city in Illium, after the war, and was killed by a tree.

(c 6002 E.D.)

"The chief of the Dust People, called as Amhadziel in our tongue, was greeted with honors by the king Indravar, he was shown the palace and the streets, but when he was loitering in the royal gardens, a great Helukmund (Banyan) reached out with its vines and choked the revered guest to death.

The king was devastated, and the Dust Men were furious. They held a trial for the tree, and found it guilty, of course. And with an axe fashioned of iron, they felled it till twas naught but a stump. They carved it out till hollow and used it as a casket for their leader. The rest of them then went back to the icy lands of the west. Strange are the ways of the Dust Men."

This concludes Appendix-A.

APPENDIX-B: OF HINNENDRAITH AND ITS FALL

In the days long past, there was a land that lay in the sea of Belfast, connecting Lüindale and Taevat. It was called Hinnendraith, from the Old Prishalavin word Hindrathis, meaning "old ghosts", as the land is now dead and gone. Hinnendraith was more fertile than Lüindale's golden fields and nyet more mystic than the lands to the north. Verily, even the great Smiths of Hjölendar claimed to have learnt their craft from the master's at Hinnendraith. Many a Tivkar lord would show genealogical tables detailing their descent from the house of the Wyrm, the mythical symbol of Hinnendraith. The continent in its heyday was a colony of the Tivkars, but about eighty years before the jewel, Tarvast, who in Kentariak is called Belfast, the sly, rebelled against the Tivkars and established Hinnendraith as a separate country, the capital of which was Stalka.

But Belfast was not satisfied. He wished to claim Taevat for his own, which meant destroying the Tivkars. And so, he bred monstrosities, picking only the most abominable of the litter. And he continued this until he made the species now called the Stalkian Drex, a humongous aquatic beast. But the creature could not be tamed and spread into the ocean. They ravaged the coasts of Hinnendraith. This, combined with attacks from the north, led to starvation and death in the land. The people of Hinnendraith begged the Eldest Folk to end these horrible things, and the Eldest Folk said:

"Thine king hast done wrong against nature, and his crime has been put on you people. We shalt let those among you flee to Taevat, where you shalt be refugees. But to those who supported these transgressions, they shalt see their home destroyed. They shalt see Hinnendraith fall to the sea."

And they were right. The Stalkian Drex caused tidal waves that laid waste to the lands. The good among the citizens were taken in by the Tivkars, and that was how the Hinnendraith

lineage continued. The Eldest Folk
safeguarded small parts of the continent,
knowing some of the future. After the land
was completely sunken and all of Stalka was in
ruins underwater, they elevated the places
they had protected, and elevated them to a
higher plane, these were the Lost Isles, the
only remaining part of Hinnendraith. But in
time, the sea levels dropped for a bit and
Hinnendraith resurfaced, and it is still here,
forming the majority of South America, where
the ruins can still be seen.

This concludes Appendix-B

APPENDIX-C: ON THE MATTER OF LANGUAGE

Language has always been a complex subject, and in the old world no less, many tribes spoke varied dialects, but there was a "common" tongue you could speak if you did not know what they spoke in the land you were in. This was Kentariak, developed in Klerova, and spread worldwide as the tongue of the free people during the War of the jewel, this is why most books were written in it, including the Ephiliostratus and most histories of Taevat and Hinnendraith. Old Prishalavin was the tongue spoken before the First Ashen War and is even more complex than Kentariak. Old Prishalavin, to a Kentariak speaker, would seem outdated. It was originally a dialect of the Tivkar language, and it is incredibly similar to it. This is why beings like Isiterok, and the Eldest Folk speak in Old Prishalavin, and that is also why I have depicted them as speaking archaic English, to give a sense of the tongue's age.

There were other languages, though not as popular, such as Lüindish, which was widely regarded as farmers' speech, and was therefore ignored by the upper classes of Lüindale. Instead, Lüindale after the war spoke a strange breed of their coarse native tongue and the flowing speech of the Prishalavin. The Tivkar language died out after their fleeing to Shivulien, but strains of it survived, one becoming Old Prishalavin as I have mentioned, and the other developing in Hilvarien and was called Hilvar, spoken by the Brozenweld especially. Hilvar was composed of block letters meant to be etched into stone, differing from the curved Prishalavin script. Inscriptions of Hilvar were found mainly at Svatlan and Kravda.

The Eldest Folk have an indecipherable language of trills and moans, suspected to be older than the sun itself. The goblins, meanwhile, speak Glimdris, a tongue with no written form. It consists of clicks, whistles, and gurgles. It was the youngest of all languages but survived for many centuries, until the last goblin was hunted down in 5600 E.D.

New Prishalavin (Kentariak) literally means "the easy speech" as it has a simple letter and word system. As it was so widespread, countless dictionaries and literary works have been composed in it. It is, therefore, the most studied out of all the languages of the old world. There have been restoration efforts to bring Kentariak back into common usage in Zimbabwe, where Illium was situated, but this proved to be as hard as getting Italians to speak Latin. If people do not learn the languages of the old world, in a few centuries, we might lose this treasure trove of knowledge to time.

This concludes Appendix-C

APPENDIX-D: OF OTHER THINGS.

Isiterok was the lord of waters, sustained by the belief and offerings of the Tivkars. They only had a few gods, most of which were elemental. There was Falytan, king of flames, Wosaterok, lord of winds, and Eravelt, master of earth. There were minor gods, such as Yavanettra, goddess of the stars, but they did not have any offerings, and therefore died out. The Tivkar God of ice, Ichenmavelt, only came to be after their coming to Shivulien. All the pantheon, except for Isiterok had their shrines and altars destroyed when Tioman was broken, leading to their demise, but Isiterok had an altar on Hinnendraith, which was now the Lost Isles, and now that they are rendered ethereal, he could never truly die. According to Tivkar belief, he is to be given a golden leaf and honey to pass through the sea of Tioman. It is believed that the sea of Tioman is now called the Atlantic Ocean, and Isiterok's domain is confined to an area of water known as the Bermuda triangle.

Goblin society is divided into strict hierarchical groups, the lowest group is the Htherik, the middle group is the Klackvick, who trade and farm, and the kingly warrior group is the Tivarik. These groups are hereditary and are so deeply ingrained into the minds of the goblin populace that they do not even wish to revolt. The Htherik work as slaves in the goblin capital of Marashtaan, (in goblin speech it is more like Mrsh-taan, but that is not very pleasant to say). There was a revolt during the war between the goblins who wished to fight against Stalhuk, and the cowards. There was a rebel goblin militarist group called the Erishtars (Ersh-trs) who hated the Kraelids and burnt down Kraelid supporting goblin cities, most notably Darimek (Dr-mek) and Renyenk (Rn-ynk). This led to a civil war, the Erishtars were defeated, but they ravaged Lüindale so badly that it had gained the name of Falenpravenca, the burning country. In the following years, goblins were classified as vermin by the Prishalavin and hunted to extinction.

There were also doings of the Prishalavin, which led to many interactions with the

Aworikwiads and the northern lands, but all that is to come after.

This concludes Appendix-D

GLOSSARY (IN ORDER OF MENTION)

Dirkwand- "dark beasts" the creatures on the earth before the sun was made.

Kirvak- "killers of life" those of the Dirkwand who immediately set to kill the new life and were defeated by the Eldest Trees.

Infandiel (Great Caves, Caves Unending)- the extremely large system of caves spreading under the world with an entrance in Taevat, houses the Dirkwand.

Eldest Trees- the trees that evolved to kill the Kirvak by producing oxygen and were killed by the Tivkars.

Stalhuk- "fair of face" the Kirvak whose body adapted to the trees. Maker of the Qhadkel, leader of The Black Army. Breaker of the world. Was imprisoned in Infandiel.

Taevat- the continent next to Klerova. Has the entrance to Infandiel and many cities such as Kravda, Svatlan and Tioman.

Tivkars- "people of Taevat" the race of people created by the trees to protect them from Stalhuk.

Freichvald- the torch made by the Tivkars to house the jewel, wrought of silver.

Jewel of Freichvald (The Jewel, The Great Jewel)- the gemstone made by the Tivkars that held the power of the first sparks of the sun, made with the wisdom of the trees.

Frikalden- lord and steward of Tioman before its destruction. Father of Amiar Stonebearer.

Tioman- the shining city of the Tivkars on Taevat, destroyed by Stalhuk.

Qhadkel- the gigantic race of stone made by Stalhuk to wage war on the Tivkars. Broke down to make the mountains of Hilvarien.

Kravda- the city of the Qhadkel in Taevat, later claimed by the Brozenweld.

Sea of Tioman- the sea that lay between Shivulien and Taevat, called so as the Tivkars crossed it after Tioman was destroyed.

Shivulien- the icy, deserted continent west of Taevat. Contained the Chayvon peaks and Hilvarien.

Amiar Stonebearer- the son of Frikalden who stole the jewel while escaping to Shivulien. Called so as he bore the jewel and kept it burning.

Hilvarien- the great city of the Tivkars in Shivulien. Later siege and taken by the Brozenweld.

Mountains of Hilvarien- the mountains formed by the broken bodies of the Qhadkel sent by Stalhuk to destroy the city.

Brozenweld- "the men of bronze" the automatons created by the Tivkars as menial workers.

Tilvuriad- the mountain underneath which Stalhuk had been imprisoned by the Tivkars.

Frdavalar- "warrior of freedom" the Brozenweld who rebelled against the Tivkars and laid siege to Hilvarien. Established the city of Svatlan.

Svatlan- "the sun capped land" the golden City made by Frdavalar on Taevat. Later became the moon.

Lüindale- the continent to the south of the planet. Famous for its shining fields and farmers. Home to the Kraelids.

Klistave- "the last people" the belief of the
people of Lüindale that they would be the only
remaining life on the planet.

Kraelid- the people who inhabit the Kraelid
empire on Lüindale.

Kraelid empire- the empire of Lüindale at the
time of the jewel.

Celethar II- father of Celvan. Reassembled the
shards of the jewel from the river Ildor.

River Ildor- the underground river into which
shards of the jewel were cast into and emptied
into a lake on Lüindale.

Celvan- son of Celethar II and was murdered
by him.

Epheltion- a Kraelid prince who found the
jewel and went on the Ephiliostratus.

Takenmerk II- father of Epheltion.

Helkara- mother of Epheltion.

Lost Isles (Isles of The Lost)- the small parts of Hinnendraith preserved and elevated to a higher plane of existence by the Eldest Folk.

Andrevel the Ship maker- the near immortal shipwright who crafted Gralakos with Epheltion.

Zilfar the wise- one of the companions of Epheltion on the great voyage. Died in a fire.

Kraizenon the bold- one of the companions of Epheltion on the great voyage. Died in a mutiny.

Htherakhton the cunning- one of the companions of Epheltion on the great voyage. Was abandoned by the crew and built the

Black Boat Ralikam. Gave rise to the race of goblins.

Gralakos- "the grain vessel" the boat of hardened grain used by Epheltion on his travels.

Docks of Klathrum- the docks on the eastern side of Lüindale.

Stalkian Drex- the monster bred by Belfast. Attacked Epheltion.

Stalka- the sunken capital of Hinnendraith. Looted by Epheltion.

Sea of Belfast- the sea beneath Klerova and a little above Lüindale.

Darvaksil- "the tome of kings" the volume of philosophical discourse between Zilfar and the spirit of Frdavalar.

Chayvon peaks- the mountain range on Shivulien and home to most of the Eldest Folk.

Ephiliostratus- the journey of Epheltion to the Chayvon peaks to retrieve the jewel.

Isiterok- the Tivkar God of the seas. Holds power in the sea of Tioman and tormented Epheltion.

Martharest- a non Kraelid city on Lüindale. Attacked by Epheltion and his crew.

Gulishta Marthero- "massacre of Martharest" the large-scale massacre of the city of Martharest by Epheltion's crew due to Htherakhton.

Black Boat Ralikam- the boat crafted by Htherakhton of his grief.

Ephelia Kristo- "the end of the Ephiliostratus" the mountain in which Epheltion was welcomed by the Eldest Folk.

The Eldest Folk (the Gray People, the Stone Men)- a species of peaceful Dirkwand. They were incredibly helpful in the events of the world. They resided in Shivulien.

Tvamiare- the boat wrought of moonlight on which Epheltion rode to the Lost Isles.

Klerova- the large continent that lay east of Taevat and Lüindale.

Prishalavin- the wizard folk of Klerova. Descendants of the Aworikwiads.

Aworikwiads- the Tivkar that lived in the northern wastes. (Not much of them is mentioned in this volume)

Tchuavak- one of the Prishalavin districts that rebelled and was destroyed.

Illium- one of the Prishalavin districts.

Fabar- one of the Prishalavin districts.

First Ashen war- the war of Illium and Fabar against Tchuavak.

Second Ashen war- the war of the districts against Ristambreda.

Ristambreda- "hall of justice" the citadel constructed to prevent battle after the First Ashen war.

Ristivals- the workers of Ristambreda.

Goblins- the filthy race of creatures said to have been born of Htherakhton' s hate and malice.

Marashtaan- the goblin capital. Later destroyed in the War Of The Jewel.

Philitria- a military fortress constructed on Shivulien.

Zomialve- a military fortress constructed on Shivulien.

Hinnendraith- the sunken continent that connected Lüindale and Taevat. Harbored the Lost Isles before its destruction.

Hjölendar- an Aworikwiad city in the north of the world. Famed for the great Smiths.

Atrexir- the demonic sword of Stalhuk forged in Infandiel.

Sthalirava- the Tchuavakian cult worshiping Stalhuk.

Ambitros- the dark mage age who brought Stalhuk back from the dead.

Battle of Grandiak- the battle that took place on Marashtaan between the Kraelids and the Black Army in which the goblin king Grandiak perished.

Glark- title given to a goblin king.

The Black Army- the Sthalirava organized into an army and controlled by Stalhuk.

Htherakhsaven- the river on Shivulien said to be made by the tears of Htherakhton.

Grilwald- the encampment of Stalhuk on the banks of the Htherakhsaven.

Djaltendreg- "dead man's dust" an ash that proves fatal when inhaled.

Dorvek of Kelvanstreng- the general who led the fortress of Zomialve.

Oltrest Shimmerspear- one of the Prishalavin soldiers who perished when attempting to break the walls of Grilwald.

Shembala- "sorry" the boat made by the enslaved Eldest Folk for Stalhuk.

Trevala- the island brought out of the sea of Belfast by Stalhuk.

Kolandrevya- the fortress of Stalhuk on Trevala.

Averiam Snow-Haired- the leader of the troops sent to cast the jewel into Infandiel.

Naestviler the Keen Eyed- a soldier who perished because of the heat in Infandiel.

Hazaltrem- the great library in Hinnendraith, burnt and destroyed.

Twakhu-al-Zamir- "the Walkers of Dust" the Prishalavin name for the Eldest Folk.

Daulimon- a city in Illium, ruled by King Indravar at one point.

Amhadziel- chief of the Eldest Folk, killed by a tree in Illium.

Indravar- king of Daulimon in roughly 6000 E.D.

Helukmund- banyan tree

Hindrathis- "old ghosts" the word from which Hinnendraith was derived from.

Wyrm (house of the Wyrm)- the royal symbol of Hinnendraith. Resembling a red, snaky beast.

Tarvast/Belfast- "the sly" name given to the king of Hinnendraith who bred the Stalkian Drex and led to the continent's downfall.

Hilvar-language developed in Hilvarien, spoken by the Brozenweld.

Glimdris- language of the goblins.

Kentariak (New Prishalavin)- speech of the Prishalavin, used almost worldwide.

Falytan- Tivkar God of flame.

Wosaterok- Tivkar God of wind.

Eravelt- Tivkar God of earth.

Yavanettra- Tivkar goddess of stars.

Ichenmavelt- Tivkar God of ice.

Htherik- lowest caste of goblins. Menial workers.

Klackvick- middle caste of goblins. Working class.

Tivarik- highest caste of goblins. Kings and warriors.

Erishtars- a militarist group that destroyed several cities and laid waste to Lüindale.

Darimek- a goblin city destroyed by the Erishtars.

Renyenk- a goblin city destroyed by the Erishtars.

Falenpravenca- "the burning country" name of Lüindale after battle with the Erishtars.

www.ingramcontent.com/pod-product-compliance
Lightning Source LLC
Chambersburg PA
CBHW021122130726
47988CB00003B/1130